# Broth & blarney
## THE IRISH EYE COOKBOOK

EDITED BY
ANNE MORRIS

READING LITHO SYSTEMS LTD

*Dedicated to my parents,*
*James and Elsie McAdden,*
*with gratitude*

*and to Sean,*
*a much-loved son*

BROTH AND BLARNEY
EDITOR: ANNE MORRIS

This edition published in 1997 by
Reading Litho Systems Ltd
6 Gresham Way, Reading RG30 6AW

ISBN: 0 9530 1620 X

Typesetting, design and reprographics by Reading Litho Systems Ltd
Printed in England by Haworth Litho Limited, London.

# Acknowledgements

I would like to thank the following people for all their help
and support in bringing this book to you:

Keith, Claire, Lizzie, Andy, Emer, James, Martin, Enda,
Sister Joseph, Simon, Seamus, Kieran and Henry.

I would also like to acknowledge the following people and
organisations for granting me permission to use extracts
from their publications:

Anvil Book Publications for *Full and Plenty* by
Maura Laverty; Barry Castle for a selection of Maura Laverty
stories; Denise Hall for *Memories of Glengariff*;
John B. Keane for *The Greatest Footballer of all Time*;
Honor Moore for *The RTE Guide Cookbook*;
The Westmeath Examiner for *A Ballinafid Octogenarian
Remembers*; Phil Brady for *A Friend We Used To Know*;
Padraig O'Toole for *Return of the Wanderer*
and William Trevor for *The Strand*.

And finally to Katrina Flanagan of the Irish Tourist Board
for permission to reproduce the colour photographs.

**95.2 & 104.1**

**BBC**

**THAMES VALLEY FM**

BRIGHTER LOCAL RADIO

- To hear Anne Morris's recipes, tune in to _**IRISH EYE**_ every Sunday evening.

- For local news, travel, weather, sport and entertainment tune in from 5am – 1am seven days a week.

- **BBC Local Radio** – serving the local community.

**BBC**

**THAMES VALLEY FM**

95.2 & 104.1

BRIGHTER LOCAL RADIO

# Foreword

When Anne Morris first told me she was going to compile this book, I must admit I didn't believe it would happen. But I had not reckoned on her boundless energy, enthusiasm, persistence and persuasive powers. After all, she had succeeded in convincing the manager of the then BBC Radio Berkshire that an Irish programme would be a good idea...something I had previously failed to do on more than one occasion.

*Broth & Blarney* is the result of more than eighteen months of hard work. The finished product has surpassed all expectations. It is a rare compilation of some of the finest Irish recipes. Uniquely, they are the favourites of celebrities and listeners to the *Irish Eye* programme alike.

Anne is originally from County Westmeath but she has lived in Berkshire for more than thirty years. For eighteen of those, she has worked for the NatWest Bank.

*Kieran McGeary*
Presenter – IRISH EYE, BBC Thames Valley FM

Anne Morris was born in County Westmeath. She was educated at Newtownforbes Convent County Longford. In 1960, Anne and her family emigrated to England. She married in 1965 and lives with her husband and family in Berkshire.

# Recipe for a recipe

How does one write a recipe?
First you need to know how to cook,
You simmer the ideas for a while,
Then pour them into a book.

The ingredients should be ready beforehand,
With poems, and pictures of Pies,
You should dump the lot into an oven,
And pray that the mixture will rise.

A balance of Warmth and Ideas,
As will be shown by a very quick look,
Causes the forming of a superbly delicious
And scrumptious Cookery Book.

By John Bishop

# Menu

# A Ballinafid Octogenarian Remembers

I was six when I had my first tooth out. The dentist came to the local sweet shop every Wednesday from nine to six. I went by myself, for both mum and dad had work to do. Tearfully I walked into that shop, clutching my sixpence and climbed into the big swivel chair.

The dentist was poised and ready to jab in the dreaded needle when the door burst open with a crash, and a huge hulk of a man stood within the framework of the door. "Take this B..... tooth out," he roared.

The dentist was as scared as I was, and politely replied "Take a seat for a moment, I'll soon be with you." "I'm not hanging around here all day. Get yer pliers and take it out now."

In 1917, language of that sort was unheard of, and a quick decision had to be made, especially as there were two ladies visible through the adjoining door. I trembled even more as the dentist said "Do you mind, Sonny, I'll do this man first."

I moved to the small chair alongside. The hulk flung himself into the high chair, and threw his head back, whilst the dentist busied himself with another needle. "What's that thing for?" shouted the big chap. "It's just a small needle, I will give you an injection and it will ease the pain." "I don't want no needle, just get the pliers and pull the B..... thing out." "I can't do that," said the dentist, "I've never done that before and must deaden the pain." "Pain, be damned. I'm in a hurry." Hesitation on the part of the dentist was followed by an even louder roar, giving the dentist no choice. In went the 'pliers' and the crunches could be heard. The tooth came without even a muscle movement from the patient.

The suggestion that he should rinse out his mouth was rejected and was followed by huge gobs of blood and slime that spattered the porcelain sink. "How much?" asked the man. Dentist: "I can't charge you for that, I've never done one like that before" wherewith the man stamped out without another word, slamming the door behind him.

# Too Many Cooks

## by Maura Laverty

Between good-natured Mary Benhan and thin-lipped Katie O'Neill there had always existed a rivalry which was due as much to their difference in character as to their widely-opposed attitude towards their calling.

They were both housekeepers. Mary looked after Doctor White. Katie was housekeeper to Mr MacNamara, the chemist.

Mary was a placid creature with a cheery smile for the world and its shortcomings. How she had managed to reach forty and still be single was a mystery which might by explained only by the scarcity of marriageable men in Killeevin, and by her whole-hearted devotion to her army of younger brothers and sisters.

She made of Doctor White's house a place for comfortable living. When the doctor invited his friends for a meal and a game of cards, he was not made to feel a criminal next day if a glass-ring marked the piano and cigarette ash powdered the carpet.

Mr MacNamara was allowed no such licence in his home. Katie O'Neill had managed to persuade the gentle timid little chemist that the house was more hers than his. There was something about the self-righteous woman, about her tightly folded mouth and gimlet eyes which would have whipped the spirit out of a man with twenty times the courage of Eddie MacNamara.

In her own way, Katie was a good housekeeper, but this was a way which made life uncomfortable for anyone using the rooms she scrubbed and polished and dusted with such relentless vigour. When Miss O'Neill came into a room and cast an eye around for signs of untidiness, poor Mr MacNamara felt he should ask her pardon for dirtying the cushions of his chair.

How was the dinner, Mr MacNamara?" Katie would ask in a tone of voice which dared him to criticise.

"Grand, Miss O'Neill – it was grand," he would stammer.

A self opinionated woman to start with, this absence of criticism finished Katie entirely. As the years went on, she came to believe that she could give lessons to Mrs Beeton.

Mary Benhan, on the other hand, had the humility of the true artist. She was willing to learn. That was why her cooking improved with every year. Why she could turn out a delicious pie, while Katie continued to make pastry of the taste and consistency of antique putty. Why her stews and gravies were fragrant with the honest essences of meat and vegetable juices, while Katie's were palette-deadening with patent bottled sauces.

When Doctor White was given a government post in Dublin, he begged Mary to go with him and look after the house he had bought in Merrion Square.

"I'd love to, doctor," she said with regret. "But I'm after living here all my life. I've all my family here, and I'd like to see my nephews and nieces grow up. No, I'll stay in Killeevin. Something will turn up for me."

Unfortunately, in a small place like Killeevin posts as housekeepers are scarce. An occasional week's work here and there was all Mary could find. She was beginning to think she had been unwise to turn down Dr White's invitation when Father John arrived for his annual visit.

The big event in Mr MacNamara'a life was the visit of his cousin, Father John for a week's shooting every autumn. When the priest's letter arrived that year, Mr MacNamara went into the kitchen with the news.

"What about meals, Miss O'Neill?" he asked diffidently. "I thought maybe we could have something – something different this year. The last time he was here we had boiled mutton the first day and cold mutton the next three days." Seeing the expression in his housekeeper's eyes, he made haste to add, "Not that it wasn't very nice, of course."

"We'll have beef, this time then," Miss O'Neill said firmly. "Roast beef the first day, cold the next, hash the day after that, and rissoles the day after that again." With the air of one announcing a great treat she added. "For a sweet, you'll get stewed prunes or stewed figs."

And that is exactly the menu which would have been served if the housekeeper had not slipped on the over-polished lino and sprained her wrist the day before Father John was due to arrive.

Mary Benhan was called in to help. "She'll manage, I suppose," Katie said grudgingly. "She should be able to make out – so long as I'm here to keep an eye on her and see that she doesn't spoil your meal with the rubbishy notions she gets out of cookery books."

Katie had to go into Kildare to have her wrist X-rayed on the day of Father John's arrival. She was horror-stricken when she came back and found that Mary had revised the menu in her absence. Instead of roasting the large joint in one piece, Mary had cut out the fillet, sliced it, dipped the fillets in the batter and cooked them in deep fat.

"That top sirloin will make a lovely little roast tomorrow," Mary said contentedly. "And the end piece can be made into a grand casserole the following day. That way, we won't have a pile of cold meat to use up. Men love hot fresh meals."

Katie was aghast. "The beautiful joint! The ignorance of you to go and chop it up like that! Why didn't you cook it the way I said? She caught sight of the rich, spicy-looking pudding which Mary was keeping hot at the back of the stove. "And what's that you are giving them for a sweet?"

"A fig pudding" "Made according to a recipe of my own. I thought it would be nicer for them than just stewed figs and custard. Honestly, Katie, I couldn't have it on my conscience to serve stewed figs to two hungry men."

Katie pounded her good hand on the table. "You're after spoiling the meal on them! I'll make it my business to go in after dinner and tell Father John and Mr MacNamara that I'm not to be held responsible."

When Katie flounced into the dining room, she found Father John in a very good humour – as any man would have been after such a meal. He had been told of the housekeeper's accident.

"Miss O'Neill," he greeted her, "I congratulate you. I've been coming to this house for years, and never before did you give us the like of that dinner. Where did you pick up all your knowledge since I was here last? Have you been studying under a chef on the sly?"

Katie gave an outraged gasp. When she recovered her breath she gave Mr MacNamara a month's notice. Surprise took away her breath for a second time, when, instead of pleading with her as he had done on such occasions in the past, he accepted the notice and offered her a month's wages on the spot.

It was no surprise to Killeevin when, six months later, Mr MacNamara made sure of enjoying Mary's cooking for life. "It's the wisest thing you ever did in your life," Father John said at the wedding.

Dr White went even further. "You're a wiser man than I was," he said. "Now I realise why I will never marry – Mary's cooking and her way of running a house spoiled me for other women. Well, good luck to the two of you."

They had plenty of it.

# Cream of cauliflower soup

1 small cauliflower
1.2 litres/2 pints stock or water
75g/3oz margarine
75g/3oz flour
500ml/1 pint milk
Salt and pepper
1 small onion, finely chopped
2 egg yolks

# Method

Cook cauliflower for 10 mins, in the boiling stock or water, adding salt to taste. Melt margarine, stir in flour and cook for 2 mins, taking care not to let it brown. Add the stock from the cauliflower, stirring well. When boiling, add the cauliflower, onion and season to taste. Simmer slowly for 40 mins. Sieve. Whisk together the egg yolks and milk in a pan and heat gently. Add to soup and stir over a low heat until thick, taking care not to let it boil. Serve with croutons.

Serves 4

# Cream of mushroom soup

25g/1oz butter or reserved chicken fat
1 medium onion – finely chopped
4 stalks celery, finely chopped
150g/7oz mushrooms, finely chopped
Pinch of dried parsley
Pinch of mixed herbs
25g/1oz flour
550ml/1 pint chicken stock
150ml/¼pt cream
Salt and Pepper

# Method

Melt butter in saucepan. Fry onions and celery over low heat until soft. Add mushrooms, herbs and seasoning. Cook until mushroom moisture evaporates. Take off heat. Mix in flour thoroughly. Add stock, stir in well, making sure there are no lumps. Bring slowly to the boil, stirring occasionally to prevent sticking. Add cream, and reheat.

Serve garnished with whipped cream and a sprig of parsley.

Serves 4

# Cream of Potato Soup

50g/2oz butter or margarine
2–3 large mild flavoured onions
450g/1 lb potatoes, peeled and cubed
850ml/1½ pints chicken stock
25g/1oz flour
1 small carton pouring cream or 5 tbls top milk
salt and pepper
parsley, chopped.

# Method

Melt half the butter in a soup pot. Cook the chopped onions, until soft and transparent over a low heat. Add the potato and cook for a further 1–2 mins. Add the stock, salt and pepper. Simmer gently until the potatoes are tender. Sieve the soup or cool slightly and put into a blender and blend smoothly. Rinse the saucepan, melt the remaining fat, stir in the flour and cook for 1 min. Add the potato mixture and cook until smooth and creamy. Stir in the cream, correct the seasoning and serve generously sprinkled with parsley.

Serves 4

This recipe is sponsored by:
## Sister Mary Joseph
in memory of my mother, Mrs Susan Martin,
who was an excellent cook of Irish meals.

# Broths

Many doubt it, but the fact remains that every North of Ireland man has a great affinity with one of our holiest saints – St Columba. That affinity is a love of broth. St Columba lived on it, and there never yet was a man born north of the Boyne who could not eat it with relish every day of his life. St Columbia's favourite pottage was Brothchan Buide, a savoury concoction of vegetable stock, thickened with oatmeal and enriched with milk. There is a story than when Lent came around the saint decided to mortify himself with ersatz broth, so he instructed the lay brother to put nothing into the broth-pot except water and nettles, with a taste of salt on Sundays.

"Is nothing else to go into it, your reverence?" asked the cook in horror. "Nothing except what comes out of the pot-stick," the saint replied sternly.

This went on for two weeks. The saint grew thinner and weaker, and the cook grew more and more worried. And then, all of a sudden, St Columba started to put on weight again and the worried look left the cook's face. The devoted lay brother had made himself a hollow pot-stick down which he poured milk and oatmeal. Thus he was able to preserve his master from starvation and himself from the horrible sins of disobedience and lies.

*Full and Plenty* by Maura Laverty

# Broth (Mutton)

850ml/1½ pints mutton stock
50g/2oz pearl barley, soaked
1 medium onion
1 carrot
1 white turnip
1 leek
Heart of a small cabbage
50g/2oz butter or margarine
Bouquet garni
Salt and pepper to taste
1x15ml tblsp parsley, chopped

## Method

Add barley, which has been soaked overnight to stock, and let it simmer, covered, while you prepare the vegetables. Chop the vegetables small, shred the cabbage finely. Melt the butter in a frying pan and saute the vegetables without browning for 3 mins. Add vegetables to stock with herbs, pepper and salt and simmer until vegetables are tender. Sprinkle with parsley.

Serves 4

# Mussel soup

1.6 litres /3 pints mussels
1 onion
1x15ml tblsp parsley
50g/2oz butter
50g/2oz flour
2 leeks
1.2 litres /2 pints milk
2x15ml tblsp single cream
1x1.25ml tsp grated nutmeg
1x1.25ml tsp pepper
1x5ml teaspoon salt
1x300ml/⅔ pint sweet cider

# Method

Place washed mussels in a saucepan with chopped onion and parsley. Add cider. Cover and place over moderate heat. Shake the saucepan frequently. Remove from heat as soon as mussels open. Strain through a fine cloth, reserving the liquor. With scissors remove beards (black weed-like parts) from mussels and place mussels on one side. Melt the butter, add the finely chopped leeks and celery and sauté for 3 mins (without browning). Stir in the milk: add pepper, salt and nutmeg, simmer for 20 mins. Put through a sieve, add liquor from mussels, cream and the mussels. Reheat and serve.

Serves 4

# Lentil Soup

1 large onion peeled and finely chopped
1 large carrot peeled and finely diced
1 stick celery finely diced
25g/1oz butter
50g/2oz leftover bacon skin, finely chopped
1 large potato, peeled and finely diced
1 tomato chopped
550ml/1 pint bacon stock
550ml/1pint water
100g/4oz lentils
1x15ml tblsp fresh parsley chopped
Freshly ground black pepper

# Method

Finely peel and chop the onion, carrot and celery. Put these in a heavy pot with the butter over a low heat. Cover and allow them to "sweat" (soften without browning) for about 10 mins. Chop up the bacon skin, the potato and the tomato. Add these to the pot and then add the bacon stock and 1 pint of water, the parsley and the pepper, and the lentils. Bring to the boil and then turn down the heat. Let the soup simmer gently for about 45 mins. If it seems too thick add more water during cooking. Serve with crusty bread. This soup will be even better the second day (keep it in the fridge overnight).

Serves 4

# Cream of celery soup WITH THANKS TO CATHAL DALY, ARCHBISHOP OF ARMAGH

25g/1oz butter
450g/1lb celery chopped, retain leaves for garnish
225g/8oz potato, peeled and diced
2 medium sized leeks, peeled and sliced
550ml/1 pint chicken stock
225ml/½ pint single cream
Salt and Freshly milled Black pepper

# Method

In a large pan melt butter over a low heat. Add celery, potato and leeks. Stir well, cover and cook over low heat for 15 mins. Add stock and salt. Cover and cook gently for 20 minutes. Purée soup by sieving or liquidising. Return to pan and stir in cream. Add pepper. Just before serving add retained chopped celery leaves.

Serves 4

# Cream of parsnip soup with mild curry

50g/2oz butter
50g/2oz flour
Combine the above in saucepan to make roux.
550ml/1pint milk
225ml/½ pint chicken stock
1 medium onion chopped
450g/1 lb parsnips, peeled and chopped
1x15ml tblsp mild curry powder
225ml/½ pint cream

# Method

Heat butter and flour in a saucepan to make a roux. Add the onion, parsnips,milk and stock. Bring to the boil, stirring all the time and cook until parsnips are soft. Purée by sieving or in a liquidiser and add the curry powder and cream. Heat gently and serve.

Serves 4

# Fish

For the proof of what a good fish dinner can do for romance there is no need to look further than Barney Malone.

Barney was a sore thorn in the side of our Fishery Board. From February to August, not a salmon in the river was safe from him. The Board had never been able to pin anything on Barney. But in a small place like ours no lawbreaker can hide his misdeeds.

Barney could not have been called a poacher in the ordinary sense. Never in a million years would he have descended to the depravity of using a net. And as for killing a female salmon during the spawning season- well, that was an iniquity no one could have laid at Barney's door. He was a decent and likeable lad. But, there it was : he was the victim of some mysterious compulsion which impelled him irresistibly towards salmon.

Barney might be walking along the river bank dressed in his best on a Sunday evening. He might be thinking of the wrongs of Ireland, or the red hair of Nellie Ryan, or of the way Nellie's father opposed the match because Barney would not stay in a steady job. He might be musing on anything under the sun except fish. But the minute he would hear a splash or see a silver gleam, into the water with him, Sunday clothes and all. Out with his gaff, then, and in next to no time the river would be one salmon less, and Barney's craving would have found temporary appeasement.

"It's a mania with him," Mr Hennessy of the Fishery Board often said. "The river draws him the way the public-house draws other men. But a stop will have to be put to his gallop. The first time we catch him, he'll go to jail."

The question was : Who was going to catch him?

That was the problem bothering Mr Hennessy as he walked along the road one evening. Old Sam Wheeler, who had been water bailiff for forty years, was due to be retired. If only we could get the right kind of man to replace him! Mr Hennessy mused wistfully. The right kind of active energetic man, a man who'd catch Malone with a salmon.

He came to the cottage where Barney's girl lived with her father, the Thatcher Ryan. He stopped and looked at the neat little house with its whitewashed walls and shining new thatch.

Isn't Malone the young fool? he marvelled. There's that grand little girl, and she's mad about him. There's a lovely home waiting for him to hang up his hat in it, if only he'd give up the poaching and get himself a steady job. There's no doubt he needs a spell in jail. It would teach him a lesson.

All of a sudden, Mr Hennessy's nostrils twitched. Through the open window of the cottage was wafted a delicious smell of a salmon frying in butter.

Mr Hennessy crept nearer the window. On a pan on the fire, two thick and rosy salmon steaks sizzled tunefully. The poacher himself was there, sitting comfortably back in his chair. With as carefree an air as if the salmon had been caught legally, Barney looked on while his girl cooked the fish.

Mr Hennessy threw open the door and walked in. "Caught at last, Malone!" he said. A legacy of ten thousand pounds would not have given him greater glee. "It's the jail for you, my lad."

Barney took it gamely. "Fair enough Mr Hennessy." He threw one leg over the other, and his face took on a happily reminiscent look. "Anyway," he said, "I had a good run for my money."

Nellie was not equipped with her lover's fortitude. She burst into tears. Through her sobs, she let Mr Hennessy know that this meant the end of her romance, that her father had sworn that Barney would never put a wedding ring on her finger if the boy ever saw the inside of a jail. She wept and entreated and begged. And the more she wept, the greater grew Mr Hennessy's embarrassment.

Even the chairman of a Fishery Board may have a flesh-and-blood heart. Even a stern official may have sufficient ordinary humanity to sympathise with the distractions of a young and pretty girl who is in love and who sees her loved one in danger of being whipped away from her. Mr Hennessy was in a difficult position. There he was with the responsibility on him ruining the happiness of two young people. At the same time, he was a conscientious man and a serious-minded man. He had to remember his duty to the Board. "I see no way out of it," he said gruffly. "The whole country knows that Malone has been asking for jail ever since he was old enough to handle a gaff."

Nellie stifled her sobs and dried her eyes. "Since you're here and since it's ready, wouldn't you have a bite to eat, Mr Hennessy?" Her voice was small and forlorn. "My share of the supper will be thrown out if you don't take it, for I'm that upset this minute I couldn't touch it for all the gold in Ireland."

The suggestion made Mr Hennessy rear back in horror. How could she imagine that he, the chairman of the Fishery Board, would share such a repast? "Have sense girl," he grunted, reaching with the tongs for a glowing coal to light his pipe.

For some reason, his pipe refused to draw for him and he had to put it back in his pocket. Maybe the way his mouth was watering was to blame. No living man could have savoured tobacco while watching Nellie Ryan dish up that meal.

Looking pathetically sad and subdued, she slithered the brown and buttery steaks on to hot plates. To the north and south of each steak she spooned little onions and baby carrots that had simmered in cream. At the east and west, she placed mealy boiled potatoes. "Let it be wasted if it must," she lamented resignedly, as she put the steaming plates on the table and filled two blue-ringed mugs with fresh butter-milk. "I'm that demented this minute, I'd choke if I tried to swallow the smallest mouthful." She sighed in a way that wrung Mr Hennessy's heart. "I'll leave now while I try to work some of the desperation out of myself by getting the fowl in for the night."

Barney Malone felt no qualms about doing justice to that supper. He pulled his chair to the table. "Even a murderer," he said, "is allowed a good feed before he goes to the gallows. Since you're sending me to jail, this will likely be the last decent feed I'll be getting for a while."

He set to. Mr Hennessy averted his eyes. He began to be very conscious of the fact that he had not eaten since mid-day.

"There's no doubt that Nellie is a prize cook," Barney commented. "This bit of salmon is done to a turn. And I always say that nothing goes so well with salmon as young vegetables done in cream the way Nellie cooks them."

Mr Hennessy swallowed. "It does seem a pity to throw out that second plateful," he said weakly. "When you think of the starving people in India, it seems a mortal sin to waste anything in the line of food."

"A deadly sin," Barney agreed. "Sit in to the table, man, while it's still fit to eat."

Mr Hennessy sat in. For ten blissful minutes, there was no sound save the satisfying symphony of cutlery and delph.

When Mr Hennessy finally pushed away his empty plate, he knew that warm glow of benevolence which always results from a satisfactory gastronomic experience.

"You're the world's biggest fool, Malone," he said, " not to take a steady job and settle down with that little girl. Nowhere in the world will you find her equal as cook."

"Nor would I find a girl to match Nellie in any other respects," Barney agreed. "But not even for Nellie would I make myself a prisoner in a factory or a shop. And if I did, I'd be doing her a wrong, for I'd end up driving her as mad as the job would drive me."

It was then that inspiration came to Mr Hennessy. "I wonder," he said, "would their be any truth in saying that you've got to set a thief to catch a thief? How would you like to be water bailiff when Sam retires next month?"

"It's the only steady job in the world that I'd want to take," Barney answered.

"But mind you, if I recommend you, you mustn't let me down," Mr Hennessy warned him. "There must be no poaching."

"I'll see to that, Mr Hennessy," said Nellie from the doorway, and their was a light in her eye which told both men that Barney's poaching days were ended.

Being the good cook she was, I am sure that Nellie would have achieved as satisfactory results with a couple of herrings.

At the knee of her Aunt Mary, who, for thirty years had been cook to a retired English colonel whose God was his stomach, Nellie had learned the Nine Commandments of fish cooking.

# Sole in cider sauce

675g/1½ lb filleted sole
A little paprika
150ml/¼ pint cider
2x15ml tblsp butter or margarine
1/½x15ml tbsp flour
125ml/¼ pint cream or top of milk
50g/2oz mushrooms, sliced
Salt and pepper
fresh parsley, chopped

# Method

Place fish in a shallow greased baking pan. If the fillets are large, cut them in half. Sprinkle with paprika. Pour cider over them. Bake the fish in a moderate oven, 350°F, 180°C, gas mark 4 for 20 mins until just tender, basting now and then with cider. When tender, remove the fillets and place in a hot fireproof dish Keep in a hot place while you make the sauce as follows:

Melt butter or margarine in a saucepan. Stir in flour. Gradually add the liquid which the fish was baked in,stir and cook until the sauce is smooth and boiling. Reduce the heat and stir in the salt and pepper to taste and cream or top of milk. Stir over a very low heat until the sauce is hot, but do not allow it to boil. Season. Add the mushrooms blanched in boiling water. Pour the sauce over the fillets. Place them under the grill for a few minutes until the sauce is bubbly and lightly browned.

Serves 4–6

# Trawlers pie

250g/1oz butter
675g/1½ lb cod fillets
Salt and pepper
30g/1½oz butter
30g/1½oz flour
275ml/ ½ pint milk
2x5ml/tsp anchovy essence
3 hard boiled eggs, chopped
Salt and pepper
450g/1 lb cooked potatoes, mashed
with milk and butter

# Method

Place cod in a buttered ovenproof dish, season. Cook for 20–30 mins in the oven 350°F, 180°C, gas mark 4. Remove fish and flake – drain liquid into jug. To make the sauce:

Add milk to make up 255ml /½ pint of liquid. Heat butter and flour in a pan, add the milk and bring to the boil, stirring all the time. Add the essence, eggs and season to taste. Pour over the fish and spread the potato on top.

Cook for 20 mins in the oven at 375°F, 190°C, gas mark 5 till golden brown.

Serves 4

# "Suir" Trout with mushrooms

4 Trout
50g/2oz flour
100g/4oz butter or margarine
100g/4oz mushrooms, sliced
250ml/½ pint cream (OR half milk, half cream)
Salt and pepper
fresh parsley, chopped

# Method

Clean, wash and pat dry the trout. Dip and roll in 25g/1oz flour, seasoned. Fry in 50g/2oz butter, until cooked through approx 15 mins. Remove and keep hot. Fry the mushrooms in the pan. Blend in flour and add cream or milk and seasoning. Bring to the boil, season. Garnish with parsley.

Serves 4

# Mock crab

1 small onion,chopped
25g/1oz butter or margarine
100g/¼ lb tomatoes, sliced
1 egg
50g/2oz grated cheese
2x15ml/ tblsp fine bread crumbs
Pinch of salt
Pepper

# Method

Gently cook the onion in butter for 5 mins, until transparent. Do not allow to brown. Add the tomatoes. Cook gently with a cover on the pan for 8–10 minutes, until the tomatoes are pulpy and the skins can be easily picked out with a fork. Add the well-beaten egg and stir over the heat until the mixture begins to thicken slightly. Do not allow to boil.

Remove from heat, add the grated cheese and stir in the bread crumbs, to give a soft, thick paste. Season. For a more savoury mock crab, add a few drops of anchovy essence – not more than 3 drops to this amount and a ½ teaspoon of mustard.

Serves 4

# Scallop Mornay

Bèchamel sauce:
275 ml/½ pint milk
½ small bay leaf
Sprig of Thyme
½ small onion,chopped
pinch of grated nutmeg
25g /1oz butter
25g /1oz plain flour, sifted
100g /4 oz cheddar cheese
6 scallops
Mashed potato for piping shells
2–3x15ml tblsp single cream
Salt and freshly milled black pepper

# Method

Make bèchamel sauce.

Put milk, bay leaf, thyme, onion and nutmeg in pan, bring slowly to boil. Remove from heat, cover with lid and allow milk to infuse for 15 minutes. Strain milk through sieve and make as for white sauce. Heat butter and flour in a pan to make a roux. Stir in the strained milk and bring to the boil. Add 50g (2 oz) cheese. Steam scallops until shells open. Remove scallop from shell and clean beard off. Wash shell. Cut each scallop in half. Line shell with a little sauce. Put 6 scallop halves into each shell. Cover with sauce. Pipe with mashed potato.

Put remaining grated cheese on top and bake in oven at 350°F, 180°C, Gas 4 for 15 minutes and brown under grill for few minutes before serving.

Serves 4

# Donegal Fish

WITH THANKS TO THE DONEGAL CHAMBER OF COMMERCE

4 Mackerel or Herring
¼ oz Butter
Oatmeal
Mustard
Salt / Pepper to taste

# Method

Take four large mackerel or herring. Gut, discarding heads and tails. Wash and dry thoroughly. Roll the fish in the oatmeal. Fry in very hot butter until golden brown. Serve with jacket potatoes and scallions.

Alternatively, if using mackerel, coat the mackerel with mustard and sprinkle with black pepper. Place under a very hot grill. Delicious with fresh soda bread and lashings of butter.

Serves 4

# A taste of Glengarriff

The endless pounding of the mighty Atlantic has fashioned a thousand peninsulas out of County Cork's rugged south-west coast-line. Deep fjords, like Bantry Bay's shelter not only the largest of ships, but fish – crab, lobster, mackerel, pollack and the mussels Bantry's becoming world-famous for.

I'm lucky enough to live about four miles outside of Glengarriff Village, gateway to the wild and lovely Beara Peninsula. It's a dramatic landscape, and its inspired many an ode to its praise including the beautiful poem Maiden in Beara, traditionally sung to the Derry Air.

Over the years, this area has seen more than its share of clan struggles, wars and starvation. Even during periods of relative calm, life was hard here. Subsistence farming on thin and stoney soil, meant a life of hard work, loneliness and isolation for many, and enforced migration for others.

But its people have nevertheless kept their humour, warmth and their welcome for the stranger. Indeed, for many years, West Cork has had the reputation of being a welcoming sort of place for those looking for a kindlier way of life.

My farm – Lickeen – borders the thousands of acres of Glengarriff's ancient woodlands and throughout the year, if you know what to look for, the woods are a rich source of berries, mushrooms, fruits such as crab-apples and blueberries, and tangy wild sorrel. In the kitchen garden, I grow potatoes, swedes, turnips, many kinds of greens and lots of herbs, including the multi-purpose comfrey, which we use for medical purposes too. Because this is, during the summer months, a busy tourist area, our local shop is well-stocked with gourmet cheeses, fine wines and a startling choice of delicacies. But nothing can beat the taste of food, particularly vegetables, that you've grown yourself. And since I don't eat meat they're particularly important in my diet.

I don't class myself as a vegetarian because I enjoy fish. And I'm glad of the opportunity to share a fish recipe created locally with you now. We use only wild salmon – the farmed kind can be oily and without that unique flavour. A five pound or so "peel" or young fish is ideal, and from June to September, they can be caught by those in the know in the serene rivers and waterways of West Cork. The potato and carrot cakes go well with this dish, as does the selection of greens which make up the salad. Maithe goile!

FOR THE SALMON: Take a cleaned and gutted young wild salmon of about five pounds. Poach the fish in a large pan with a handful of peppercorns, a small chopped onion, a bay leaf and one cup of gorse wine. (If you can't make you're own, O'Neills of Kerry make a fine one). Add enough water so that the liquid just covers the fish and simmer gently until flesh is tender.

FOR THE SALAD: Mixed greens, to include spinach, corn salad and sorrel, washed and torn. Pour over a dressing of cider vinegar, unrefined honey and mustard to taste, whisked together vigorously. Then toss.

FOR THE CAKES: 3 large carrots, grated. 3 medium potatoes, peeled and grated. Half a cup of minced onion. 3 eggs, lightly beaten. Quarter of a cup of sifted flour. Salt and pepper to taste. 2 tablespoons of chopped parsley. Mix all ingredients together thoroughly and spoon on to a hot buttered griddle. Cook until golden brown on both sides. Serve with sour cream or plain yoghurt on top.

BLASKET ISLANDS, CO KERRY

COOLEY MOUNTAINS, CO LEITH

# Escalope of Salmon with Tarragon butter sauce

WITH THANKS TO DANIEL O'DONNELL

100ml/4 fl oz Dry white wine
150ml/6 fl oz fish veloute
20 fresh tarragon leaves, finely hopped
50g/2oz unsalted butter
4 x 125g/5oz escalopes of salmon
1 x15ml /tblsp olive oil
Salt and freshly ground white pepper

# Method

Reduce the white wine to a syrup, add the fish veloute and the tarragon and leave to infuse for a few minutes. Slowly beat in the butter. Meanwhile season the salmon and fry in the oil in a non stick pan for 2–3 minutes on each side. To serve, pour the sauce into the centre of 4 warm plates and place the salmon on top.

Serves 4

# Warm scallops with Asparagus and chive cream sauce WITH THANKS TO THE AMBASSADOR EDWARD BARRINGTON

12 large scallops, sliced in half
8 green asparagus, cut in half and split lengthways
50g/2oz Irish cheddar (grated)
1 shallot chopped
250ml/½ pint of fish stock
425ml/¾ pint Double cream
2x15ml tblsp chives,chopped
½x5ml tsp lemon juice
2x15ml tblsp sesame oil
8 chives cut into batons
125ml/5 fl oz white wine

# Method

Place asparagus in boiling salted water for 1 minute. Remove and keep warm. Sauté scallops in a hot pan with 1 tblsp sesame oil for 1 minute. Remove and keep warm. Add chopped shallots to pan, white wine, fish stock and reduce by two thirds. Add cream and whisk in grated cheese. Leave to simmer over a gentle heat. In a frying pan, heat 1 tblsp sesame oil. Add lemon juice, seasoning and chopped chives to cream sauce. Add scallops and poach for one minute.

Toss asparagus in the hot frying pan for 1 minute and season. Divide scallops and chive cream sauce between 4 warm plates. Spoon warm asparagus on top of the scallops. Sprinkle with baton chives. Serve with green salad and hazelnut dressing.

Serves 4–6

# Fish and Green sauce WITH THANKS TO WILLIAM TREVOR

4 fillets plaice (or sole)
Dijon mustard
Mix together:
1x15ml tblsp fresh breadcrumbs from a
stale loaf, finely crumbled
1x15ml tblsp parsley or dill, finely chopped
½x15ml tblsp freshly grated parmesan
cheese
(A little oil or melted butter)

# Method

Preheat oven to 180°C, 350°F, Gas No.4 . Wash and dry fish. Put into a
greased oven-proof dish. Spread mustard thinly on fillets, press
breadcrumb mixture thinly on top and put in oven for 5–15 mins,
according to thickness of fillets. Take out before fish begin to shrink
away from skin edges. Sprinkle with oil or melted butter and place under
grill until brown and crisp ( a few minutes). Serve with lemon or green
sauce.

# Green sauce

Whip together 2 small dark green courgettes and either smoked salmon
pate or smoked salmon pieces (or, if preferred, 1–2 anchovies). Add a
teaspoon, or more to taste, of whipped cream. Add pepper and a
squeeze of lemon.

Serves 4

# Meats

by Maura Laverty

According to Charles Laughton, Henry the Eighth thought nothing of devouring a shoulder of lamb at one sitting. He couldn't hold a candle to Head Mooney at home in our place. Head belonged to people who were notorious throughout the County Kildare for their passion for pig's head. They earned plenty of money on the canal boats and on the bog, but they never had a penny to show for it. All their good earnings were squandered on pig's head. When the boy I'm talking about got married – Paddy, he was called then – his wife was full of a bride's eagerness to please. Knowing the family failing, off with her into the town when she got the first week's wages into her hand on Saturday, and she spent the best part of it on the biggest pig's head in Miss Regan's shop. "It'll last us the week", she planned. She had it nicely cooked and bolstered on white cabbage for Paddy when he came in from Second Mass the next day.

Paddy sat down, blessed himself and started in. Wrapped up in it, he continued with the good work until his wife, who had a normally healthy appetite, could stand it no longer. "What about me, Paddy?" she said diffidently. "Aren't you going to cut a little bit for me?"

Paddy looked up in shocked amazement. "And do you mean to tell me, girl," he demanded, "that you didn't cook e'er a one for yourself?" It was then she christened him Head, and the name never left him.

# Calves liver with Irish Whiskey and tarragon

WITH THANKS TO VAL DOONICAN

250g/8oz calves liver
25g/1oz butter
3x15ml tblsp of Irish Whiskey
100ml/4 fl oz of beef stock
1 clove of garlic,crushed
½ small carton single cream
1x15ml tblsp freshly chopped tarragon

# Method

Heat the butter in a frying pan. Coat the liver in seasoned flour, fry gently until pink. Remove the liver to a heated plate, then pour the whiskey into the pan.

Light with a match (stand back!) and let the flames die down before adding the garlic, stock and tarragon. Allow the sauce to reduce a little before adding the cream. Boil until the sauce thickens, then pour over the liver. (add a little salt and black pepper if necessary).

Serves 2

# ICA Pork stew

450g/1 lb pork
25g/1oz plain flour
Salt and pepper
1 green pepper, seeded and sliced
1 onion, chopped
1x15ml tblsp vinegar
1 chicken stock cube
2–3x15ml tblsp oil
2 large cooking apples, peeled and sliced
250ml/½ pint water
½x5ml tsp soya sauce
250ml/½ pint cream

# Method

Cut the pork into 1-inch cubes. Heat the oil and fry the onion until lightly brown. Remove from pan. Toss meat in seasoned flour. Fry until brown all over. Put meat and onion in a casserole dish. Mix in any remaining flour, 250ml/½ pint water, pepper, apples, vinegar, soya sauce and chicken cube. Season to taste.

Cover and cook for 2½ hours at 350°F, 180°C, gas mark 4. Stir in cream, before serving with glazed carrots and boiled potatoes.

Serves 4-6

**Note:** You could use less than the full half-pint of cream, which makes this a very rich dish.

# The Greatest Goalkeeper of our Time

**M**onuments are never erected to the type of man I have in mind. His words are never quoted and his opinion rarely sought. When he dies only a few will mourn him.

But perhaps my picture is not too easily recognisable so I will try to draw the man accurately – and the only way to do that is to create a situation. This is the type I have in mind....

First of all, take any given Sunday in summertime. He gets out of bed. He shaves. He dons his sportscoat, flannel pants, and sandals and goes downstairs to a breakfast which inevitably consists of a rasher, an egg and a sausage. He is not feeling too well but he puts the breakfast where it belongs all the same.

He glances through the papers and goes to Mass. He doesn't go too far up the Church but he doesn't stand at the door either. After Mass he stands at the nearest corner for a few minutes. He meets a man just like himself. They enter a nearby public house together.

In the public house the customers are talking about a football match. The local team are playing a challenge game in a village several miles away. Our man goes home to his dinner of roast beef, peas and potatoes. He has a good stroke with a knife and fork and is no joke when it comes to making spuds disappear.

After dinner he is between two minds – whether to go to bed or take out his bicycle and go to the football match. The stout and the heavy meal have made him drowsy but the instinct of the sportsman is strong within him. An uncle of his was once a substitute for the North Kerry juniors and a cousin of his mother's was suspended for abusing a referee.

Our hero duly arrives at the football pitch. The crowd is small as this is a game of little consequence. He parks his bicycle and pays a shilling admission fee. The teams are taking the field.

The familiar jerseys have brought his loyalty to the surface but he notices a discrepancy in the side. He counts only fourteen men and then, suddenly, he hears his name being called.

The first faint suspicion dawns on him but he pretends he doesn't hear. Casually he begins to saunter to the other end of the field but the voice, pursuing him, grows louder. He increases his gait but the unmistakable call arrests him:

"Hi Patcheen! Will you stand in goals?"

He can run away now and be forever disgraced in the eyes of his neighbours, or he can stand and be disgraced anyway. His coat is whipped off and, before he knows it, there is a jersey being pulled over his head. He hears a disparaging comment from some onlookers on the sideline:

"Good God! Look what they have in goals!"

His blood is up. He thrusts his trousers inside his socks and tightens his shoelaces. He takes up his position and the game is on. He is not called upon to do anything during the first half or during the second half either. There is little between the teams but what little there is stands in favour of our man's team.

A high lobbing ball drops into the square. The backs keep the forwards at bay and our man goes for the ball. He gets it – only barely, but the important thing is that he gets it. The forwards are in on top of him. He's down. He holds on to the ball like a drowning man and for the excellent reason that he has nothing else to hold on to. He hears a rending sound. His flannel trousers are torn. One of his shoes is pulled off his foot. Someone has a hold of his tie and is trying to choke him. He is kicked in the shin and he receives a treacherous wallop in the eye. There must be a hundred men on top of him!

Then the whistle sounds and he is able to breathe freely. He is safe now and here, at last, is the great opportunity. He rises with the ball in his hands. He hops it defiantly and then, in one of those great moments which only happen once in a lifetime, he goes soloing down the field.

The whistle blows again but he pretends not to hear it. Then he stops and turns and with a tremendous kick aims the ball straight back at the referee. Dignified, he returns to his goals with his torn flannels flapping behind him and his tie sticking out from the back of his neck like a pennant on the lance of a crusader.

Nobody offers him a lift after the game. He cycles home to his supper of cold beef and bread and butter. He changes his clothes and makes no attempt to conceal the black eye.

He combs his hair and walks down to the corner. He meets his pal and they stroll leisurely towards the public house.

Our man calls for two pints and, settling himself comfortably on his stool, launches into a detailed account of the save. If he adds a little it is understandable – and if he had been wearing togs and boots heaven only knows what would have happened.

The important thing is that he wasn't found wanting when his time had come. He made no headlines but he didn't disgrace himself either. The football scribes will not mention him when the annals of the great are being compiled but in the eyes of his compeers and in consideration of the porter he had drunk and of the dinner he had eaten I think he must surely be reckoned among the great goalkeepers of our time.

By John B.Keane

# Braised Breast of Lamb

WITH THANKS TO THE GALWAY
CHAMBER OF COMMERCE

2½–3lbs lean breast of lamb (boned)
1 lb mixed diced vegetables – carrots,
turnips, celery, onion
1 pint water or clear stock
¼ ounce carrageen moss
(steeped and strained)
seasoning to taste

# Method

Get the butcher to bone the breast of lamb. Season, roll up and place on a dry pan or a rack in a hot oven (220°C) for 15 minutes. Pour off all the fat from the pan and add half the water. Cover, reduce heat to 180°C and cook for a further 40 minutes. Place diced vegetables in the pan and add remainder of the water, cover and cook for a further 45 minutes. Place meat on a hot dish and arrange vegetables around it. Prepare the gravy by boiling rapidly to reduce to a third. Remove any fat, add the carrageen moss and simmer for 5 minutes. Strain and serve.

Serves 4-6

# Irish stew "Main Guard"

900g/2 lbs lamb (neck or cutlets)
225g/8oz sliced onions
225g/8oz sliced carrots
2 sticks celery, chopped
1 white turnip, peeled and chopped
900g/2 lbs sliced potatoes
Salt and pepper
Stock or water

# Method

Trim fat from meat. Place a layer of sliced potato in the base of a casserole dish. Season lightly. Add a layer of meat and sprinkle on the vegetables. Repeat layers finishing with potatoes. Barely cover with stock. Cover casserole and cook slowly for 2½ hours at 350°F, 180°C, gas mark 4. Skim away any excess fat. Sprinkle with parsley.

Serves 4

# Lamb braised with wild garlic

WITH THANKS TO
DARINA ALLEN

leg of young lamb
oil, butter or lamb fat
salt and freshly ground black pepper
3–6 wild garlic plants, picked preferably
just before they flower
450g/1lb scallions, peeled
450g/1lb small potatoes, peeled

# Method

Set the oven to 180°C, 350°F, gas mark 4.

Brown the lamb in a little oil, butter or lamb fat. Season with salt and freshly ground black pepper. Chop up the wild garlic plants and press into the skin of the meat with the herbs (if used). Sauté the scallions and potatoes in the same fat and then put them around the meat and herbs in a heavy cast iron casserole. Cover with a tight fitting lid.

Cook in the oven for 1½ to 2 hours or until cooked through. Strain off the juices and pour off the fat. Serve the juices separately as gravy. A little good stock may be added if not enough juices are left in the pot. More chopped fresh herbs may be added to the gravy.

Note: later in the season, garlic cloves can be used with fresh herbs, such as thyme or marjoram, making a good substitute for the garlic's own green leaves.

Serves 4-6

# Chicken with Tarragon

6 chicken breasts
juice 2 small lemons
2 tsp paprika
1 large garlic clove
1 tblsp chopped tarrigon
50g/2 oz butter
12–14 sun-dried tomatoes
0.5pt double cream
cayenne pepper
bunch of rocket

# Method

Slice chicken crossways into thin strips. Mix together the lemon juice, paprika, garlic and tarragon in a large bowl and add the chicken turning to coat, cover leave at room temperature for 1 hour.

Melt butter, add chicken and cook gently for 8/10 minutes stirring occasionally.

Cut sun-dried tomatoes lengthways into ¾ pieces using slotted spoon. Then transfer chicken to a plate and set aside. Bring pan juices to the boil and cook rapidly for about 2 minutes reducing slightly. Stir in cream and bring back to boil for 2/3 minutes. Then season with salt and cayenne pepper.

Add the chicken to the pan and most of the sun-dried tomatoes. Bring to the boil and simmer gently for 2 minutes, spoon into a shallow dish and cover loosely. Then proceed to keep warm in a low temperature oven.

Serves 6

# Limerick loin of lamb

1 loin of lamb
– ask butcher to remove bone
Black pepper
10 strips of orange rind
10 leaves of rosemary
50g/2oz seasoned flour
1 beaten egg
Toasted breadcrumbs

Sauce:
Juice from cooked lamb
Remaining orange rind
Juice of orange
4x15ml tblsp dry sherry
Sprig rosemary
Sprig thyme
4x15ml tblsp redcurrant jelly
Salt and pepper

# Method

Trim nearly all fat from lamb. Arrange rosemary and orange strips along fillet of lamb. Pepper, roll and tie with string. Roll lamb in seasoned flour, brush with beaten egg and roll in breadcrumbs.

Heat oven to 400°F, 200°C, gas 6 . Melt dripping in a roasting dish, and when very hot put in lamb and brush all over with dripping. Cook for one hour.

Remove lamb and skim fat from the cooking juices.

To make the sauce, put lamb juice, remaining orange peel, orange juice, sherry, rosemary, thyme, redcurrant jelly, salt and pepper into a saucepan. Bring to the boil and strain. Slice the lamb, spoon over sauce. Garnish with twirls of orange

Serves 4-6

# Pork casserole

4 good sized pork chops
1 tin tomatoes
Garlic salt to season
Paprika pepper
1x15ml tblsp oil
1 large onion,chopped
1x Small pkt frozen peas
1x5ml tsp Italian seasoning
1x15ml tblsp tomato purée
1 stock cube (pork or beef)

# Method

Fry pork chops on both sides in hot oil until browned, add the onion and cook for a further 5 mins. Place chops in casserole dish. Pour over the tomatoes and add the frozen peas.

Season with salt and pepper according to taste. Add tomato purée and stock cube. Cover casserole with a tight fitting lid and bake in oven at 350°F, 180°C, gas 4 for approx. 1–1¼ hours. This dish is best served with baked potatoes.

Serves 4

# Cheddar style pork chops

100g/4oz cheddar cheese
100g/4oz mushrooms
125ml/¼ pint unsweetened apple juice
25g/1oz butter
4 pork chops
4x15ml tblsp breadcrumbs

# Method

Butter a large, shallow oven-proof dish. Wash and chop mushrooms and arrange over base of dish. Season well with salt and pepper. Trim fat on chops and place on top of mushrooms. Pour on apple juice.

Mix finely grated cheese and breadcrumbs together and sprinkle on each chop. Bake in hot oven (400°F, 200°C, gas mark 6) for about 45 minutes until pork is tender and top is golden and crisp.

Serves 4.

# Longford lamb

450g/1lb Cooked lamb (leftover is best)
1 tin chopped tomatoes
1 onion, chopped
1 clove of fresh garlic, crushed
Salt and pepper
Rosemary and Thyme
550ml/1pint cheese sauce
6 medium potatoes

# Method

Heat a little oil in a pan add the onion and garlic and fry gently for 5 mins. When onion is soft add rosemary and thyme. Cube lamb, add tin of tomatoes and lamb to onions in pan. Bring to boil then simmer. Meanwhile, boil the potatoes, then slice and deep fry.

Finally, put layer of potatoes in bottom of casserole dish, then layer of lamb mixture, then cheese sauce. Repeat until all mixture is used up. Make sure last layer is potatoes. Put in pre-heated oven 350°F, 180°C, gas mark 4 for 30 minutes,or until top layer is golden brown.

Serves 4.

# Pork steak studded with apricots and topped with apple and cinnamon stuffing bound in puff pastry

Stuffing:
2 large cooking apples, peeled and sliced
1 onion, chopped
1 clove garlic, crushed
½ stalk celery, chopped (optional)
1 glass cider 125ml
1x5ml tsp cinnamon
250g/8oz breadcrumbs
450g/1lb puff pastry

# Method

Slice a thick pork steak down the middle. Stuff with a line of dried apricots. Fold back together again and set aside. Blanch some green vegetables, ie. spinach, savoy cabbage, leeks, etc. Set aside.

Fry onion, garlic and celery (if being used) in a little oil. Add the apples with cider and cook until cider has almost evaporated. Add the cinnamon. Cook until quite dry. Mix in the breadcrumbs. Cook until the breadcrumbs are crispy.

Top the pork steak with green vegetables and stuffing. Surround with puff pastry and glaze. Bake at 400°F, 200°C, gas 6 for 30 minutes, reduce heat to 300°F, 150°C, gas mark 2 and bake for 40–60 minutes.

Serves 4–6

# Garlic Chicken

4 Chicken breast portions
2x15ml tblsp butter or oil
1 large packet of garlic boursin cheese
150ml/5 fl oz sour cream
1 clove of garlic, crushed
2x5ml/ tsp arrowroot or cornflour
175ml/6 fl oz white wine
Salt and pepper

# Method

Gently brown chicken in butter in a pan. Mix the boursin with sour cream. Add garlic into mixture and blend in arrowroot and wine. Pour over chicken to cover. Simmer for 1 hour until chicken is tender. Season to taste.

Serves 4

# Gammon steaks with whiskey sauce

WITH THANKS TO DOREEN WILLIS

4 gammon steaks
2x15ml/tsp finely chopped onion
1x15ml/tblsp brown sugar
1x15ml/tblsp whiskey
25g/1oz flour
50g/2oz butter,melted
150ml/¼ pint water or stock
Salt and pepper to taste

# Method

Brush steaks with half the melted butter, and grill for 7–8 minutes each side. To make sauce, gently fry onions in remainder of butter until cooked. Remove from heat and stir in flour, gradually, add stock. Return to heat. Add sugar and bring to boil. Simmer gently for about 2 minutes to cook flour. If sauce seems a little thick, add more water. Add whiskey and season to taste.

Place gammon steaks on a warm serving dish and pour on sauce. Serve with peas, carrots and sauté potatoes.

Serves 4

# Pigeon in Cassis

WITH THANKS TO HENRY YELF

4 pigeon breasts
seasoned flour
5 shallots, chopped
1x15ml tbs ground nut oil
1x10ml tsp juniper berries, crushed
knob of butter
125ml/15fl oz white wine
4x10ml dsp cassis

# Method

Slice pigeon breasts in half. Toss in seasoned flour, fry the shallots in a pan for approx.1 minute. Add the breasts and brown on each side for 5 minutes. Add the juniper berries, butter, white wine and cassis. Simmer for 10 minutes. Place into an ovenproof dish and cook in the oven for 20 minutes at 350°F, 180°C, gas mark 4.

Serves 4

# Wexford stuffed lamb

WITH THANKS TO KATHLEEN HINCHY

900g/2 lb boned shoulder of lamb, trimmed of excess fat.
½x5ml tsp salt
½x5ml tsp black pepper

**Stuffing:**
25g/1oz butter
1 small onion, finely chopped.
1 small carrot, scraped and finely chopped

100g/4oz raisins, soaked for 20 minutes in 4x15ml tbsp orange juice
1x5ml tbsp fresh, chopped parsley
50g/2oz fresh breadcrumbs
1x15ml tsp grated lemon rind
1x125ml tsp ground cinnamon

# Method

Preheat oven to 350°F, Gas mark 4, 180°C. Place the meat on a working surface and sprinkle with salt and pepper.

To make the stuffing: In a small frying pan, melt the butter over a moderate heat. When the foam subsides, add the onion and carrot and fry, stirring occasionally for 5–7 minutes or until the onion is soft, but not brown. Remove from heat.

Place the onion and carrot mixture and the cooking juices in a bowl, add raisins with orange juice, parsley, breadcrumbs, lemon rind and cinnamon. Mix the ingredients well together.

Spread the stuffing over the meat. Roll up the meat and tie with string to secure it.

Place the meat in a roasting tin and place in the oven. Roast the meat for 2–2½ hours or until the juices run out when the meat is pierced. Remove the tin from the oven.

Cut the meat into thick slices and keep warm. Serve with juices over meat and vegetables.

Serve with mashed potatoes, peas and beans.

Serves 6

# Fillet of beef with red wine sauce

WITH THANKS TO THE ROSCOFF RESTAURANT, BELFAST

500g 1lb 2oz oxtail
Salt and freshly ground black pepper
50g/2oz unsalted butter
50g/2oz shallots, finely chopped
25g/1oz carrots, finely chopped
25g/1oz celery, finely chopped
25g/2oz mushrooms

750 ml/1¼ pints red wine
500 ml/17 fl oz meat stock
1 bouquet garni
4 x 175g /6oz fillet of beef trimmed
500g /1 lb 2oz pomme purée

**To garnish:**
2 spring onions, trimmed and sliced into fine rings

# Method

Pre-heat the oven to Gas mark 4, 180°C, 350°F.

Trim the oxtail of all sinew and fat. Cut into segments and season with salt and pepper. Cook the oxtail in half the butter, in a braising pan, until nice and brown all over. Add the shallots, carrots and celery and mushrooms, cook lightly and then add the red wine and boil to reduce by half. Add the meat stock and bouquet garni and bring back to the boil. Skim off the scum. Cover and braise in the pre-heated oven for 2 hours. Remove the oxtail and flake the meat. Set aside in a warm place. Skim the stock and pass through a fine sieve.

Fry the beef fillets gently in a heavy pan with the remaining butter for 3 minutes each side. This depends on the size and shape of the fillets and how you like your meat. Set aside on a wire rack to rest for several minutes.

To assemble, place the pomme purée in the centre of warm plates. Place the fillets on top. Carefully place the flaked oxtail over the beef, sprinkle on the sliced spring onion. Spoon the seasoned sauce around the pomme purée.

Serves 4–6

# Vegetables and Salads

The way Lottie Fenlon hated onions was a great hardship on Hugh Doherty.

"Miss Fenlon has agreed to take you as a boarder," Father Molloy told Hugh when he first came to Ballyderrig to oversee the renovation of the church. "She's a grand cook. You'll be comfortable with her."

At 50, good cooking and comfort were very important to Hugh. Lottie bore out the priest's recommendation. In return for his two ten a week, her boarder got a good fire, a good bed, a comfortable armchair and the pleasant companionship of his gentle-voiced landlady. Her soda-bread was feather-light, her roasts dripped juice, and she had a way with sauces that could transform the most pallid bit of boiled cod into a fast-day feast.

For Hugh, her cooking had one big lack. She never used onions. Hugh was partial to onions. He liked them fried as his mother used to cook them. Not the grease-sodden discoloured strings which so many women pass off as fried onions, but those crisp, golden-brown rings, tender and succulent, which you get if the rings are separated, tossed in seasoned flour or dipped in batter, and then fried for 3 minutes in boiling fat.

There were few dishes he liked more than boiled onions, smothered in cheese sauce, topped with breadcrumbs and browned in the oven. He adored baby onions chopped small and added with hot milk and a lump of butter or margarine to fluffy mashed potatoes. Given his choice of supper-time sandwiches, he would swear that there was nothing to beat buttered wholemeal bread and thin slivers of Spanish onion, well-seasoned.

But Lottie would not let an onion in the house. The reason was psychological. Onions had been responsible for the wrecking of her first and only romance. It happened twenty years before when she was 17 and in love with a bank clerk called Cecil Quin, a very refined young man who would have died rather than be seen in the street without his yellow gloves and walking stick.

Lottie's romance crashed the evening she had onions for tea before meeting Cecil for their bi-weekly walk along the canal bank. If Mrs Fenlon had lived long enough to tell her daughter the facts of life, Lottie would have known that, provided proper precautions are taken, a girl may eat an acre of onions without fear of alienating her boy friend, however refined. She would have been taught that a glass of milk sipped slowly or a mouthful of parsley chewed leisurely will destroy all evidence of onion-eating.

But poor Lottie was an uninstructed orphan. When, on that fateful evening, Cecil bent to give her one of his carefully-rationed kisses, she was hurt and dismayed to see him rear back offendedly. He left her with a quick goodnight and never took her out again. A year later he married Angela Murphy, who was as refined as himself and who had a good dowry into the bargain. To complete Lottie's humiliation, Angela told all Ballyderrig of the solecism which had killed the bank clerk's love. From that day Lottie tuned her back on men and on onions.

After Hugh came to board with her, he made quite a few tentative suggestions regarding the culinary uses of onions....that though steak was good with mushrooms, it was even better with onion rings...that stuffing was not the same, somehow, without onions.

Lottie froze him. "If you want onions, Mr Doherty," she said, her voice trembling, "I'm afraid you will have to find accommodation elsewhere. Inside this house an onion will never come!"

After that, he put up with the lack of his favourite vegetable, feeling that Lottie's house afforded compensations with atoned. She was glad he stayed. Since his coming she had discovered that a woman who lives alone can be very lonely.

When he had been with her about three months, Lottie had to go to Dublin to see about a tooth that was worrying her. "I won't be able to get a bus back until the morning," she told him. "If I leave you to look after yourself for the night, will you be alright?"

Hugh assured her that he could manage. Just the same, she was worried. When she walked into Father Molloy in Dublin that evening, she was glad to accept his offer of a lift home.

When she stepped into her beeswaxed hall, she stopped dead and sniffed. There was no mistaking the smell. Onions were being cooked in her kitchen.

She threw open the kitchen door. There was Mr Doherty, one of her aprons tied around his ample middle, happily engaged in basting something that sent its aroma through the house. At her step, he turned quickly and dropped the spoon. Guilt and dismay made his flushed face several shades redder.

"I'm – I'm sorry!" he stammered, hanging his head. "I – I was making stuffed onions the way my mother used to do them."

There was something in the big man's apologetic humility, in the disarray of his wispy fair hair and in his sacred blue eyes which awoke latent maternalism in Lottie Fenlon. All at once, the anger left her. The bitterness of years went from her. It was replaced by something soft and warm which made her look ten years younger.

Hugh Doherty saw the transformation. In some peculiar way, it made him stop feeling like a schoolboy caught stealing apples. Instead, he felt like a masterful man. He acted like one too. In two strides he was across the kitchen and had Lottie in his arms.

For their betrothal supper they ate the stuffed onions. Luckily, Hugh had cooked enough for two.

# Colcannon

900g/2 lb cooked potatoes
454g/1 lb cooked kale
Small bunch of spring onions
250ml/½ pint cups milk or cream
Sprig of parsley
100g/4 oz butter
Salt and pepper

# Method

From Dublin to Shannon
They all love Colcannon
And no-one has known it to fail.
It's a dish of great fame
And in Irish, its name
Translated, means White-Headed Kale.

This favourite of mine
Has spring onions, chopped fine
And boiled up with milk or with cream.
The potatoes then mash
As quick as a flash –
With chopped buttered kale they're a dream.

Beat them all up together
Till they're light as a feather
Then pile on some more knobs of butter.
When the whole lot is topped
With parsley, fine-chopped,
Oh, what cries of delight they will utter.

Serves 4–6

# Savoury potato pancakes

100g/4oz mashed potato
4x15ml tblsp self-raising flour
1 egg, beaten
1 onion, grated
1–2 rashers cooked bacon
1x15ml 1 tbsp chopped parsley and chives
Good pinch of mixed herbs
1 tomato, chopped
Some green pepper (optional)
Salt and pepper
Milk to mix

# Method

Combine the potato and egg, adding the flour with enough milk to make a soft batter. Add the other ingredients as available. Drop tablespoon of the mixture into shallow fat or oil in a frying pan. Cook until bubbling on one side: turn and brown on the other side. Serve with eggs, sausages, bacon or fried black and white pudding.

Warning: don't serve them to anyone who is a martyr to indigestion or you won't be popular...

Serves 4

# Kinsealy onion pie

18cm (7") short pastry pie shell, baked
50g/2oz butter or margarine
175g/6oz cheddar cheese, grated
2 large onions, thinly sliced
1 green pepper (optional)
3 eggs, beaten
Salt and pepper
425ml/¾ pint milk

# Method

Melt the butter or margarine in a pan and slowly cook the sliced onions until soft and golden. Add the finely chopped or minced green pepper, removing the core and the seeds first. Put into the pie shell and sprinkle with cheese. Bring the milk to boiling point. Whisk the eggs with salt and pepper, add the hot milk gradually, beating well. Pour over the onions and cheese. Bake in a moderate oven (350°F, 180°C, gas mark 4) for about 25 minutes until the filling has set.

Serves 4–6

# A Friend We Used To Know

Each day we take the paper up, and glance its pages through,
to find out if there's something strange or if there's something new;
And as we look, we're stunned to see where death has struck a blow,
and in silence there, we breathe a prayer, for a friend we used to know.

Perhaps 'twas at a football match, or later in the bar,
we cracked a joke and sang a song, when we had had a jar:
We used to meet quite often, then, as people come and go,
we went our ways and he became a friend we used to know.

Or, maybe, it's the girl we met on holiday
when hand in hand we strolled the beach or danced the hours away;
We came to know each other well – but such is life: – and so,
we went our ways and she became a friend we used to know.

How crowded are our thoughts, as now we go down 'memory lane',
and there, in blissful dreaming, we live through life again:
But now another link has snapped – yes, one by one they go –
How very few now left, of all the friends we used to know.

Vain and empty is this world, when all is said and done;
however long – how short the years – until life's race is run;
Then, when the sands of time run out, and to eternity we go;
may someone, somewhere, breathe a prayer, for a friend they used to know.

# Irish stuffing

WITH THANKS TO J. HAWESHAW

900g/2 lb potatoes
250g/9oz smoked bacon
2 medium sized onions
100g /4oz butter/margarine
Sprig of parsley
1 stick Celery (optional)
Pepper

## Method

The ideal substitute for boring mashed potatoes. This dish is the perfect accompaniment for poultry especially turkey.

Boil potatoes and mash with butter and chopped parsley. Stir bacon, finely chopped onions and celery over a low heat for 5–10 minutes. Mix ingredients together in a bowl and add generous amount of pepper. Place ingredients in an ovenproof dish and reheat Gas mark 6,400°F, 200°C for 30 minutes.

Serves 4–8 people depending on appetite!

# Pan Boxty

WITH THANKS TO KIERAN MCGEARY

450g/1 lb potatoes, peeled and grated
175g/6 oz plain flour
1/2x5ml/ tsp baking powder
¾x5ml/ tsp salt
125ml/4 fl oz milk
Cooking oil

# Method

Sieve flour, salt and baking powder together. Mix with grated potatoes. Add milk to make a thick batter. Heat frying pan. Have it well oiled. Pour batter on to pan and cook on either side for 3–4 minutes, or until golden brown. Serve hot with butter and a little sugar.

Serves 4.

# The Strand.

You can walk along the strand all the way from Ardmore to the derelict one-storey Georgian house on the cliff. You pass Ballyquin on the way, a little cove that has a car-park now. The sand is smooth and damp, here and there marbled with grey, or dusty dry, depending on whether you choose to walk by the sea or closer to the cliffs. There are shrimps and anemones in the rock pools, and green slithery seaweed as you pass the rocky places by. The cliffs are clay, easy game for the encroaching winter waves. Washed timber and plastic bottles are the flotsam of the shingle.

A woman pushes a bicycle, the buckets that hang from its handlebars heavy with seafood from the rocks. A horse and cart carries gravel or seaweed back to Ballyquin. In the nineteen thirties this strand was always empty, except on the rare days when the dark figure of a priest was seen, suddenly out of nowhere, clambering down the cliff-face. Clothes were weighed down with a stone and then he ran naked to the sea.

Inland a little way, not always visible from the strand, is Ballyquin House, four-square and architecturally simple, cream-washed when the O'Reilly's lived there. Mrs O'Reilly, a widow, attired always in black, was a woman whose unobtrusive presence called for, but did not demand respect. All the old decencies were in the woman that Mrs O'Reilly was: you hardly had to look at her to know she would rather not live at all than live dubiously, in some mean-spirited way. Her two children, Biddy and Henry, were in their early twenties. Her brother, a silent man who kept his hat on, worked on the farm. An old uncle - known as Blood-an'Ouns because he so often used the expression - got drunk in Ardmore every Corpus Christi, but otherwise did not touch a drop.

Henry O'Reilly was known locally as the laziest man in Ireland, but in my childhood opinion he was also the nicest. Red-haired and already becoming bulky, he took me with him on the cart to the creamery and on the way back we would stop at a cross-roads half-and-half - a shop that was a grocery as well as a public house. He had a bottle of stout himself, and bought me a lemonade and biscuits. He would settle his elbows on the counter, exchanging whatever news there was with the woman who served us. 'Give the boy another mineral,' he'd say, and he'd order another packet of biscuits for me, or a Cadbury's bar. Eventually the horse would take us slowly on, lingering through the sunshine, Henry O'Reilly having a nap, the reins in my charge. Most of the day it took, to go to the creamery and back.

Henry O'Reilly made me an aeroplane, nailing together a few scraps of wood, which he then painted white. He showed me how to snare a rabbit and how to shoot one. When I was eight or so I weeded field of marigolds with him, a task that didn't require much energy because we stopped whenever a new story began, and Henry O'Reilly went for stories: about his ancestors, and '98, and the Troubles, the Black and Tans, the time Michael Collins passed nearby. At twelve O'clock we returned to the farmhouse and sat down in the kitchen to a meal of potatoes, which were tumbled out on to a newspaper in the centre of the table.

The O'Reilly's land stretched right to the cliff edge, but the O'Reillys rarely ventured on to the strand, as country people who live by the sea so often don't. There were cows to milk, and feed to be boiled for the hens, and crops to be harvested, the churns of milk delivered. The front door of the house was never opened, the rooms on either side of it and the bedrooms above only entered when dusting took place. Gladstone hung in severe majesty over a mantelpiece, eyed by the Virgin above the door. Hall and stairway were embellished with further reminders, faith kept, thanks given.

There is a glen where the strand ends, separating the land that was once the O'Reilly's from woods that have become dense. And there, much closer to the cliff edge than the O'Reilly's, is the derelict house. The woods stretch for miles behind it and somewhere in the middle of them lived a man with rheumy eyes called Paddy Lyndon. In a tumbled down outbuilding there was an old motor car with brass headlamps - one of the first, Paddy Lyndon averred, that had taken to the roads in Ireland. 'Are you sober, Paddy?' Henry O'Reilly would always greet Paddy Lyndon when they met, an enquiry that received no response.

Glencairn House the derelict place was called when first I knew it fifty years ago. It was owned then by an Englishman who'd left Ireland during the Troubles and only rarely returned - a Mr Fuge who'd built a dream house, not knowing that dreams are not to be trusted. 'As good a man as ever stood on two feet,' Paddy Lyndon said. 'A man that never owed a debt.' Through the cracks of the efficiently boarded windows nothing could be distinguished in the darkness that kept the rooms' secrets. A briar rose trailed through a patch of garden, gone as wild as the surrounding gorse. I liked the mystery of this good Englishman who's left his property in Paddy Lyndon's charge, who only stayed for twenty minutes when he came back. 'There's stories about Fuge I could tell you,' Henry O'Reilly said, but he never did because he never got round to making them up.

But it is the sea, not houses or people, that dominates the strand. To the sea, and the sand and rocks that receive it, belongs the images you carry with you when you pass on to the woody slopes of the glen, and the barley fields. The waves call the tune of the place, in a murmur or a passionate crescendo. There's salt on the inland air, and seagulls strut in the furrows.

Jellyfish float in when they're in the mood for it. Once in a while there's a trawler on the horizon. The sea on the turn's the best, the sand left perfect waiting to be doused. It's easier to skim pebbles over the water when it's unruffled - as it was the time I nearly drowned, causing panic one hot afternoon.

Two generations on, the shells are as they've always been; so are the paw-prints of a dog. The dog has a branch of brown seaweed trailing from its jaws, and takes no notice when he's called. People nod as they pass, or say hello. Children build castles and watch them being washed away, old men paddle. A primus stove splutters. It's out of the question that a naked priest will run into the sea.

Still no one lives in the derelict house. The boards that once so curtly covered the windows, a kind of packing case around the house, have fallen away. You can see the rooms now, but if ever there was furniture all of it has gone. The wall beside the avenue has collapsed.

The O'Relly's farmhouse is different too. Years ago Biddy made her way to Chicago, Henry married into Ardmore. Mrs O'Reilly and her brother, the old man too, are long since dead. The house is no longer in the family, the land is differently farmed.

There is no nostalgia here, only remembered facts - and the point that passing time has made: the strand is still the strand, taking change and another set of mores in its stride, as people and houses cannot. While you walk its length, there is something comforting in that.

CLIFFS OF MOHER, CO CLARE

CONNEMARA PONY TRAIL, MANNIN, CO GALWAY

BALLYDONEGAN BAY, BEARA PENINSULA, CO CORK

Newtowncashel Cottage Museum, Co Longford

# Potatoes O'Brien

700g/1½ lbs potatoes, cooked,
peeled and diced
1 medium onion,chopped
½ pepper, chopped
Knob of butter
100g/4oz grated cheese
1x15ml/tblsp flour
Pinch dried parsley
Salt and pepper
3x15ml/tblsp cream

# Method

In a frying pan soften onion and peppers in butter. Add flour, parsley, salt and pepper to diced potatoes and mix. Then mix in softened onions and peppers. Spoon half the mixture into baking dish and cover with half of grated cheese. Add remaining potato mixture and cover with the rest of the cheese. Pour cream over the cheese and bake for 45–60 minutes until golden brown,at 375°F,190°C, gas mark 5.

Serves 4.

# Champ

6–8 potatoes, unpeeled, eg. Golden Wonders or Kerr's Pinks

100g/4oz scallions or spring onions (use the bulb and green stem) or 45g/1½ oz chives

300ml/12 fl oz milk

50–100g/2–4oz approx. butter (according to taste)

Salt and freshly ground black pepper

# Method

Scrub the potatoes and boil them in their jackets for approx 15 minutes. Finely chop the scallions, spring onions or chives. Cover the scallions with cold milk in a pan and bring slowly to the boil. Simmer for about 3 to 4 minutes, then turn off the heat and leave to infuse. Peel and mash the freshly boiled potatoes and, while hot, mix with the boiling milk and onions. Beat in some of the butter. Season to taste with salt and freshly ground black pepper. Serve in one large or four individual bowls with a knob of butter melting in the centre. Serves 4.

**A) Parsley champ**

Add 2–3 x15ml tblsp freshly chopped parsley to milk, bring to the boil for 2 or 3 minutes only, to preserve the fresh taste and colour. Beat into mashed potato and serve hot.

**B) Chive champ**

Substitute freshly chopped chives for parsley

**C) Dulse champ**

Soak a couple of fists of seaweed in cold water for an hour or more. Drain and stew in milk until tender, about 3 hours. Add a good knob of butter and some pepper and beat into the mashed potato. Taste and correct the seasoning. Serve hot.

**D) Pea champ**

This special champ could only be made for a few weeks when the fresh green peas are in season. Cook the green peas in the boiling salted milk with a pinch of sugar until tender. Add to mashed potatoes and pound together in the usual way.

# Spicy stuffed vegetables

4 red peppers
3–5x15ml/ tbsp oil
1 onion,chopped
2-3 garlic cloves, chopped
½x5ml tsp black mustard seed
½x5ml tsp cumin seeds
1 chilli, chopped
6 mushrooms chopped
Lots of chopped coriander
200g/8oz boiled rice

Fry the onion and garlic until soft, then add seeds, and the rest of the mix, and cook for a further 5 mins,use to fill the red peppers. Pour over rice. Season to taste.

**For the sauce:**

½x15ml tblsp oil
½x5ml tsp mustard seed
½x5ml tsp cumin seed
1 onion, chopped
2 cloves garlic, sliced
1 tin chopped tomatoes
1 tin tomato purée
1–2 sliced chillies
Coriander leaves

Heat the oil in a pan, add all the ingredients and cook for 5–10 minutes. Arrange the filled peppers in the sauce. Cover and simmer for 20–30 minutes.

Serves 4.

# Pandy

900g/2 lb floury potatoes, unpeeled
Butter
Creamy milk or fresh single cream
Salt and pepper

# Method

A light fluffy mashed potato dish often made for children or older people if they were feeling unwell.

Boil the potatoes in boiling salted water until just cooked, peel immediately and mash with lots of butter. Season with salt and freshly ground black pepper to taste and then whip in some of the cream. It should be light and fluffy. Eat while hot.

Serves 4–6.

# Return of the Wanderer

(After 7 years teaching in Africa, an Aran Islander goes home)

The narrow road wound itself like a frayed ribbon along the edge of the cliffs. Sturdy stone walls pinned it to the ground as if to stop the winter gales blowing it away. Here and there along the roadside and dotted among the rocky nooks stood whitewashed cottages acting like kingpins pegging the wavering ribbon more firmly to the barren hillside. And at the bottom of the hill, beside the sea, lay Onaght village with its stonewalled church brooding over the gurgling bay.

I grew up regarding Onaght church as my church, a mile or so from Bungowla, the village where I was born. Bungowla itself is the westernmost and indeed the bleakest village of the Aran Islands. Nestling among the grey rocks at the bottom of a steep cliff, the village sits squattily at the end of the island road, its eleven houses clinging like limpets to the bare landscape as if trying to hide itself from the hostile elements. Because it is at the end of the road, nobody comes to Bungowla by accident and hence it is a quiet place disturbed only by the murmur of winter sea periodically punctuated by the wailing call of a sea bird or by a dog baying at the moon.

Like the morning mist that sometimes creeps in from the Atlantic, a strange peace often hovers over the village and hugs the wild shoreline. It is this peace that I find so refreshing, and indeed inspiring, after the strife and civil wars of Africa, which I've weathered now for several years. I don't miss the humid heat.

It was my first day home and as I walked along the road towards Onaght church, the wind was at my back pushing me forward. It hurled huge raindrops after me, some of them missing their mark to splutter against the limestone walls or splash noisily on the dull grey flagstones. A westerly gale was in the making. Huge waves swept in from the Atlantic, rolling dourly eastwards towards the Irish mainland. Already, angry breakers were baring their crests like white teeth against the edges of our island's jagged rocks as if impatient to eat into our few remaining fields and devour our very homes. It was almost night-time.

Onaght church was empty and getting dark. The red light flickering near the alter gave a semblance of light, warmth and even refuge from the elements if not from the world at large. I soaked in the lone quietness. I needed it. And yet, it was only and island of imagined quietness in a sea of sound with wild nature's choir entertaining from a distance. It was not easy to leave Africa behind but here in Aran, on my first day back, salty raindrops replaced sweat on my brow. The breakers falling on the shore ground out a slow rhythmic beat. Winter's gale blew over the island and whistled its wailing hymn all around me like some gigantic stereophony.

I did not feel any of those sounds a distraction and the mood of the returned exile followed me home as I drifted thoughtfully westwards along the meandering road to Bungowla. By now night was pitch dark. The sea, by the sound of it, was angrier. Peering into the night, I could make out the white edges of the breakers crashing towards the shore. By now the gulls and other sea birds had wisely taken to the shelter of their homes in the southern cliffs and all sensible people too had gone indoors. The rain had stopped. However, the wind and sea insisted on keeping up their lamentation, a weirdly overlapping duet, occasionally made more piercing by the screech of a stray cormorant caught out, like myself, in the storm. A faint light showed in some island houses and the moon was starting to peep warily over the eastern horizon, casting a pale ghostly polish on the wet countryside and giving a sticky feeling to Galway Bay.

Goodbye Africa. I was home in Aran at last. Rounding the bend in the road, facing the Atlantic, Eeragh Island lighthouse flashed its bright beam into my face. It pierced the wet empty night of the sea, checking if the world was still there and casting a cold knowing eye on life, on Galway Bay and on me.

Padgaig O'Toole

# Country herb soda bread

200g/8oz plain flour
200g/8oz wholemeal flour
1x5ml/tsp salt
1x5ml/tsp baking soda
25g/1oz butter or margarine
2 large onions, grated
1x15ml tblsp mixed herbs
2x15ml tblsp chopped parsley
250ml/½ pint buttermilk or
250ml/½ pint milk
2x5ml tsp lemon juice
50g/2oz finely grated cheddar cheese

# Method

Sieve the flour, salt and baking soda into a bowl. Mix in the wholemeal flour. Rub in the butter (or margarine) and add the onion, parsley, and herbs. Mix well. Add enough buttermilk (or milk plus lemon juice) to mix to a fairly soft dough. Turn on to a floured surface and knead into a round. Flatten out 9" across and set on a floured baking sheet. Mark the top into 8 wedges. Brush over with a little sweet milk and sprinkle with the grated cheese.

Bake in a pre-heated hot oven, 400°F, 200°C, gas mark 6, for 30–35 minutes until the bread sounds hollow when turned up and tapped on the base. Serve with warm soup, or buttered and sandwiched with slices of corned beef, plus a cup of soup, as a cold day snack.

# Apple cake

2 cooking or eating apples, peeled, cored and finely chopped

125g/5oz self-raising flour

a pinch each of nutmeg, ground, cloves, and salt

75g/3oz caster sugar (less for eating apples)

50g/2oz butter plus a little extra for greasing tin and for topping

1 egg beaten

1 tblsp milk

demerara sugar

# Method

Grease well a 7–8″ tin. Preheat oven to 190°C/375°F/Gas Mark 5. Sift the flour with the nutmeg, cloves and salt. Rub in the butter until the mixture resembles fine breadcrumbs. Stir in the apples and caster sugar. Now add the egg and just enough milk to make a soft dough. Press the mixture into the tin and dot the top with tiny pieces of butter. Finally sprinkle demerara sugar over the top. Bake for 20–30 minutes until springy to the touch. If in doubt, test with a skewer which should come out clean. The cake will look brown and glossy. Serve warm with or without cream or vanilla ice cream. It is also good served cold for tea.

# The engineers cake

200g/8oz plain flour
200g/8oz currants
200g/8oz sultanas
100g/4oz lemon peel
100g/4oz butter
100g/4oz soft brown sugar
1x5ml/tsp ground ginger
1x5ml/tsp mixed spice
1x5ml/tsp baking soda
2 eggs
125ml/4fl oz milk

# Method

Mix together the dry ingredients. Melt the butter. Add it with the beaten eggs and milk to the dry ingredients. Mix well together. Pour into a greased and lined 450g/1 lb. loaf tin. Bake at 350°F 180°C, gas mark 4, for 1½ hours.

# Whiskey cake

350g/12oz mixed dried fruit
60ml/4 tsp whiskey
175g/6oz butter
175g/6oz soft brown sugar
grated zest of 1 orange
3 eggs, beaten
225g/8oz plain flour
5ml /1 tsp baking powder
5ml /1 tsp mixed spice
50g/2oz ground almonds

# Method

Soak the mixed fruit in the whiskey overnight. Preheat oven to 170°C, 325°F, gas mark 3. Grease and base line a 20cm/8" cake tin. Cream the butter and sugar until fluffy. Add the orange zest. Gradually beat in the eggs. Sift the flour, baking powder, salt and mixed spice and add to the egg mixture with the fruit and whiskey and the ground almonds. Turn the mixture into the cake tin and bake for 1½-hours.

Variation: Cover the top of the mixture with halved glace cherries and sprinkle with demerara sugar before baking, to give an attractive crunchy topping.

# Syllabub.

2x15ml tbsp lemon juice
75g/3oz caster sugar
150ml/¼ pint white wine
2x5ml tsp lemon rind,grated
250ml /½ pint fresh double cream
50g2oz bar milk chocolate,grated

# Method

Mix the wine, lemon juice, rind and sugar in a bowl. Cover and allow to stand for 3 hours to allow the flavours to combine. Whisk the cream until it is beginning to thicken, and gradually pour in the wine mixture, beating until stands in soft peaks. Put into glass dish sprinkle with grated chocolate and chill before serving.

Serves 4.

# Rhubarb cheesecake

10 digestive biscuit,crushed
50g/2oz butter,melted
25g/10z caster sugar
450g/1lb rhubarb,trimmed and cubed
4x15ml tbsp,orange Delrosa or orange concentrate
75g/3oz sugar
2 eggs, beaten
200g/8oz cottage cheese, sieved
100ml /¼ pint cream,whipped
mint leaves to decorate

# Method

Make the biscuit crust by combining biscuits, butter and sugar. Press into a 20cm/8" round tin. Leave to cool.

Cook the rhubarb with orange Delrosa and sugar in a pan until soft. Leave to cool and add the eggs, cook over a low heat until it thickens. Allow to get cold and stir in the cottage cheese and whipped cream. Taste and add more sugar if necessary. Pour onto the biscuit base and chill till firm. Decorate with mint leaves and pieces of rhubarb before serving.

Serves 4–6.

# Mary's lemon cheesecake

200g/8oz digestive biscuits,crushed
50g/2oz caster sugar
60g/2½oz butter
450g/1 lb Philadelphia cheese
1 lemon jelly
Rind and juice of a lemon
1 packet dream topping
100ml /4 oz milk

# Method

Melt butter and add crushed biscuits and sugar. Mix well and spread on to base of loose-based cake tin (20cm/8"). Bake for 8 minutes at 180°C, gas mark 4, 350°F. Allow to cool.

Dissolve jelly in 250ml / ½ pint of water, add fresh grated lemon rind and juice and stir in made up topping (following instructions on the packet). Beat cheese until fluffy and stir into the mixture. Allow to set slightly and pour onto biscuit base. Refrigerate and serve chilled.

NB: There is a lot of mixture and it can quite easily be made up into 2 cheese cakes. One for now and one can be put into the freezer and eaten at a later date.

Serves 4–6.

# Blackberry and apple tart

450g/1 lb approx. puff pastry

3–4 cooking apples eg. Bramley, Seedling or Grenadier

100g/4 oz blackberries

150–175g/5–6oz white caster sugar, depending on the sweetness of the apples

3 or 4 cloves, crushed

Beaten egg to glaze

Fine caster sugar

## Method

Roll out half the pastry and line a 25 cm/10 inch Pyrex plate. Trim the excess pastry, but leave about 2 cm/¾ inch overlapping the edge. Peel and quarter the apples, cut out the cores and cut the quarters in half (the pieces of apples should be quite chunky). Put the apples on to the pastry and pile them up in the centre. Put the blackberries on top, leaving a border of 2.5cm/1 inch around the edge. Sprinkle with sugar, then add the crushed cloves to taste.

Roll out the remainder of the pastry, a little thicker than the base. Wet the 2.5 cm/1 inch strip around the tart and press the pastry lid down on to it. Trim the pastry, again leaving a 5 mm/¼ inch edge. Crimp up the edges with a knife and then scallop them. Make a hole in the centre to allow steam to escape. Brush with beaten egg. Roll out the pastry trimmings and cut into leaves to decorate the top of the tart. Brush with egg wash.

Bake in a hot oven at 250°C, 475°F, gas mark 9 for 15 to 20 minutes, then turn the heat to moderate for a further 40 to 45 minutes, depending on how hard the apples are. Test the apples to see if they are cooked by inserting a skewer through the hole.

Serve hot sprinkled with soft brown sugar and softly whipped cream.

Serves 4–6.

# Bananas and whiskey

WITH THANKS TO MARY O'HARA

8 bananas
25g/1oz butter
Juice of 1 lemon
50g/2 oz dark brown sugar
3x15ml tbsp whiskey
Cream to serve

# Method

Peel and halve the bananas. Arrange in a well-buttered dish. Mix lemon juice with 2x15ml tbsp of water and pour over fruit. Sprinkle with sugar. Bake in a moderately hot oven, gas mark 5, 375°F, 190°C for 20 minutes. Add the whiskey and cook for another 2 minutes.

Serve hot with lots of cream.

Serves 4.

# Guinness pudding with whiskey sauce

100g/4oz sultanas
100g/4oz raisins
100g/4oz currants
2x5ml tsp grated orange rind
100ml/4 fl oz orange juice
225ml/8 fl oz Guinness
100g/4oz whiskey
300g/11oz wholemeal breadcrumbs
3 eggs, lightly beaten
100g/4oz plain flour

1x5ml tsp ground cinnamon
1x5ml tsp baking powder
**Sauce:**
100g/4oz butter
50g/2oz demerara sugar
50g/2oz golden syrup
2x15ml tbsp whiskey
225ml/8 fl oz single cream
whipped cream or ice cream to serve

# Method

Place sultanas, raisins, currants, orange rind and juice, Guinness and whiskey in a bowl, cover and leave to stand overnight.

Grease a 3lb capacity pudding steamer (or two smaller ones) with melted butter. Fold breadcrumbs through fruit mixture and leave to stand for 5 minutes, stir in eggs, then sifted flour, cinnamon and baking powder.

Spoon into prepared pudding steamer, lower into boiling water and steam for 2 hours. Leave to stand for 15 minutes before turning out of steamer.

**To prepare sauce**

Place butter, sugar and golden syrup in a heavy-based pan, stir until sugar dissolves, cook for 1 minute then add whisky. Stir through cream and remove from heat. Pour sauce over hot pudding. Serve with whipped cream or ice cream. Serves 4–6.

# Caramelised apple tart with vanilla ice cream

WITH THANKS TO MARLFIELD HOUSE WEXFORD

600g/5oz puff pastry
1 egg beaten with 1x15ml tbsp Caster sugar 'egg wash'
6 large apples
50–75ml / 2–3 fl oz Calvados
Juice 1 lemon
90g/3½oz butter
115g/4½oz ground almonds
6 large scoops of vanilla ice cream

# Method

Roll 12 discs 5½ inches across, place 6 on a tray cut a 4½ inch disc in the other one. Egg wash first discs, place the 6 rings on top as neatly as possible, sprinkle almonds into each one.

Peel and slice apples into quarters, reserve.

Boil sugar, Calvados and lemon juice, whisk in cold butter.

Slice apple quarters into 5, place neatly inside tarts using one apple for each tart, brush with syrup.

Bake at 250°C, 475°F, gas mark 9 for 10 minutes, then brush with more syrup, bake for another 5 minutes. Serve with 1 large scoop of ice cream.

Serves 4–6.

# Irish Soda Bread

300g/12oz plain flour
½x5ml tsp salt
½x5ml tsp bread soda (bicarbonate)
½x5ml tsp cream of tartar
275ml/½pint buttermilk
(If buttermilk is not available, sour milk
may be substituted. To sour fresh milk,
add half a teaspoon of lemon juice or
vinegar to one pint of milk and leave in a
warm place for 10–15 minutes).

# Method

Mix dry ingredients together and sieve twice to incorporate plenty of air.
Make a well in the centre of the flour and add enough buttermilk to get
an easy-to-handle, soft but not wet dough. Knead very lightly, form into
a round and mark with a cross. Bake in a hot oven 230°C, 450°F, Gas
mark 8 for 20 minutes. Reduce to 200°C, 400°F, Gas mark 6 for a further
20 minutes.

# Porter Cake

450g/1 lb sifted cake flour

450g/1 lb brown sugar

450g/1 lb seedless raisins (half raisins and half currants can be used instead)

250g/8oz sultanas

1x5ml tsp bicarbonate of soda, melted in warm Guinness

4 eggs

200g/½ lb butter

100g/4oz glace cherries, chopped

100g/4oz blanched, chopped almonds

100g/4oz mixed, chopped peel

275ml/½ pint Guinness, warmed

grate rind of 1 lemon

Pinch of mixed spice

# Method

Rub the butter into the flour and add all the other ingredients, blend well. Beat the eggs with the lukewarm Guinness and add the bicarbonate of soda. Mix this well into the dry cake mixture, and turn into a greased and lined cake tin, measuring 21cm/9" in diameter and 9cm/3" high.

It should be covered with greaseproof paper, and bake in a slow oven (325°F, 175°C, gas mark 3) for about 3 to 3½ hours, removing the paper for the last half hour. Test with a skewer before removing from the oven. It makes a good Christmas Cake, and if iced will keep well in a tin.

# Rich Chocolate Cake

175g/6oz plain good quality (dark) chocolate
100g/4oz caster sugar
1/2x5ml tsp almond essence
175g/7oz ground almonds
100g/4oz butter or margarine
4 eggs (size 2) at room temperature
4x15ml rounded tsps flour

# Method

Lightly grease a spring-clip tin 23cm (9") diameter and line the base with baking parchment. Preheat the oven to 180°C, 350°F, Gas mark 4.

Melt the chocolate and allow to cool a little. In a separate bowl, beat the butter until soft, then beat in the caster sugar. Then beat in the eggs one at a time, adding 1 rounded teaspoon of flour with each one (the mixture will curdle somewhat). Stir in the almond essence and the melted chocolate and the curdling will disappear. Then stir in the ground almonds. Put into the tin and spread out. Bake in the oven for 50 minutes until cooked. Partly cool in the tin on a wire tray, then remove from the tin and cool completely.

# Chocolate Icing

125g/5oz plain good quality (dark) chocolate
25g/1oz butter
150ml/5 fl oz fresh cream
50g/2oz icing sugar

# Method

Melt the chocolate, butter and cream together. Stir in the icing sugar and allow to cool (to thicken).

**To ice the cake**

When cold, spread apricot jam over the top and then spread the chocolate icing on top of it, allowing some to dribble down the sides. Decorate the top with grated chocolate.

# Wholemeal Cheese Scones

200g/8oz wholemeal flour
200g/8oz self raising flour
1/4x5ml tsp salt
1x5ml heaped tsp baking powder
Black pepper (freshly ground)

100g/4oz grated cheddar cheese
2 large eggs, beaten
100ml/¼ pint milk
1x5ml tsp mustard

# Method

Put the flours, salt and pepper, baking powder and the grated cheese in a bowl and mix together the eggs and milk and add to the dry ingredients to make a moderately soft dough. Turn out onto a floured surface and knead lightly. Roll out the dough in a rectangular or square shape, about 3.5 cm (1½") thick. Use a sharp knife and cut into about 12 square (or rectangular) scones.

Place on a greased baking tin and bake for about 25 minutes at 200°C, 400°F, Gas Mark 6 until golden brown and well cooked.

NOTE: A special finish can be given to scones by brushing with milk or beaten egg and sprinkled with sesame seeds – before cutting dough into squares.

# Fruit Dessert

1pkt sponge fingers
tinned fruit -or fresh (pears, peaches,
mixed fruit or raspberries all work well)
275ml/½ pint of whipping cream
2x15ml tblsp demerara sugar

# Method

Line a fire-proof dish with sponge fingers. Soak with fruit juices. Add whatever fruit being used. Cover well with whipped cream – making sure the edges of the dish are sealed. Put in fridge for a short time. Just before serving cover cream with the demerara sugar. Place under a hot grill until the sugar caramelises – this will happen very quickly. Serve immediately.

Serves 4.

# Never fail cake

450g/1 lb mixed dried fruit
200g/8oz sugar
100g/4oz butter
200g/8oz self-raising flour
2 eggs, beaten
150ml/¼ pint water

# Method

Put all the ingredients (except the flour and eggs) into a saucepan and simmer for 15 minutes. Cool the mixture, stir in eggs and flour and pour into a greased loaf tin. Cook for 1½ hours at 170°C, 325°F, Gas mark 3.

# Chocolate biscuits

100g/4oz plain flour
1x15ml tbsp cocoa
Pinch salt
100g/4oz butter or margarine
50g/2oz caster sugar
Vanilla essence

# Method

Lightly grease a baking tray. Preheat oven to 190°C, 375°F, Gas mark 5. Sieve the flour, cocoa and salt. Beat the butter, sugar and essence until light and creamy. Add half the flour and cocoa and mix thoroughly. Add remaining dry ingredients and mix well. Roll into small balls, place on baking tray. Flatten with fork dipped in cold water. Place in oven and cook for 10–15 minutes.

When cold sandwich together with butter cream.

**Butter cream:**

25g/ 1oz butter

50g/ 2oz sieved icing sugar

Soften butter, add icing sugar and beat until light and creamy.

# Bible cake

200g/8oz Judges 5:25 Last Clause (Butter)

200g/8oz Jeremiah 6:20 (Sugar)

1x5ml tbsp 1 Samuel 14:25 (Honey)

4 Jeremiah 17:11 (Eggs)

250g/10oz Samuel 30:12 (Raisins)

100g/4oz Nahum 3:12 (Figs)

75g/3oz Numbers 17:8 (Almonds)

350g/14oz 1 Kings 4:22 (Flour)

1x5ml tsp 11 Chronicles 9:9 (Spices)

1x5ml tsp Amos 4:5 (Yeast)

A pinch of Leviticus 2:13 (Salt)

5x5ml tbsp Judges 4:19 (Milk)

# Method

Grease and line a 23cm, 8" round cake tin. Beat Judges 5:25 (last clause), Jeremiah 6:20 and 1 Samuel 14:25 until light and fluffy and creamy. Beat in Jeremiah 17:11 gradually, beating well after each addition following Soloman's advice in Proverbs 23:14 (beat well).

Stir in 1 Samuel 30:12, Nahum 3:12 and Numbers 17:8. Mix 1 Kings 4:22, 11 Chronicles 9:0, Amos 4:5 and Leviticus 2:13, then fold into the mixture with Judges 4:19.

When thoroughly blended, spoon the cake mixture into the prepared tin and bake for 2½ hours at 170°C, 325°F, gas mark 3. Leave the cake to cool in the tin. Turn out and wrap for several days before cutting.

# Barm Brack

300g/12oz flour
200g/8oz sugar
300g/12oz dried fruit
½x5ml tsp baking powder
1x5ml tsp mixed spice
1 egg, beaten
300ml/½ pint hot tea

# Method

Soak the fruit overnight in tea. Add beaten egg and sugar to the fruit and tea. Sift together flour, spice and baking powder and add to fruit mix. Bake in a greased 22–23cm,7–8" square tin for 1½ hours at 180°C, 350°F, Gas mark 4. Cool in tin. Serve buttered.

# Chocolate Mars biscuits

100g/4oz margarine
¾ packet rich tea biscuits, broken
50g/2oz handful raisins
2x15ml tbsp syrup
1 Mars bar

# Method

Melt margarine and Mars bar and add syrup. Heat a little. Mix in the biscuits and raisins. Pour into an oiled tin and leave to set.

# Celtic shortcake

WITH THANK TO SUSAN ANDERSON

250g/10oz plain flour
150g/6oz butter
100g/4oz caster sugar
50g/2oz semolina

# Method

Rub butter and flour together. Add sugar and semolina and mix well. Press mixture into a flat tin, preferably with a push out bottom. Prick all over with a fork. Place in oven at 180°C, 350°F, gas mark 4, for 35 minutes. Remove from oven and leave for 5 minutes then sprinkle sugar over the top and cut into pieces. Eat while warm for best results.

# Irish Christmas Cake

200g/8oz butter
200g/8oz soft brown sugar
4 eggs, lightly beaten
250g/10 oz plain flour
2x15ml tbsp mixed spice
200g/8oz seedless raisins
200g/8oz sultanas
100g/4oz mixed peel
100g/4oz chopped walnuts
8–12x15ml tbsp Guinness

# Method

Cream butter and sugar together until light and fluffy. Gradually beat in the eggs. Fold in the flour and mixed spice. Mix well together. Stir 4 tablespoons of Guinness into the mixture and mix to a soft dropping consistency. Turn into a prepared 22cm, 7" round cake tin and bake in a very moderate oven (170°C, 325°F, gas mark 3) for 1 hour. Then reduce heat to cool oven (150°C, 300°F, gas mark 2) and cook for another hour and a half. Allow to become cold. Remove cake from the tin. Prick the base of the cake with a skewer and spoon over the remaining 4–8 tablespoons of Guinness. Keep the cake wrapped in greaseproof paper for one week before eating.

# Irish Coffee

WITH THANKS TO EILISH DONOGHUE

Cream – Rich as an Irish brogue
Coffee – Strong as a friendly hand
Sugar – Sweet as the tongue of a rogue
Irish Whiskey – Smooth as the wit of
The land.

# Method

Gradually heat a steamed whiskey goblet or handled tankard. Pour in one jigger of Irish Whiskey – the only whiskey with the smooth taste and full body needed. Add 3 cubes of sugar. Fill the goblet with strong black coffee to within one inch of the brim. Stir to dissolve sugar. Top off with cream. Do not stir after adding cream as the true flavour is obtained by drinking the hot coffee and Irish Whiskey through the cream.

# The Deserted Village

Sweet was the sound, when oft at evening's close
Up yonder hill the village murmur rose;
There, as I pass'd with careless steps and slow,
The mingling notes came soften'd from below;
The swain responsive as the milk-maid sung,
The sober herd that low'd to meet their young;
The noisy geese that gabbled o'er the pool,
The playful children just let loose from school;
The watchdog's voice that bay'd the whisp'ring wind,
And the loud laugh that spoke the vacant mind;
These all in sweet confusion sought the shade,
And fill'd each pause the nightingale had made.
But now the sounds of population fail,
No cheerful murmurs fluctuate in the gale,
No busy steps the grass-grown foot-way tread,
For all the bloomy flush of life is fled.

Oliver Goldsmith
1730–1774